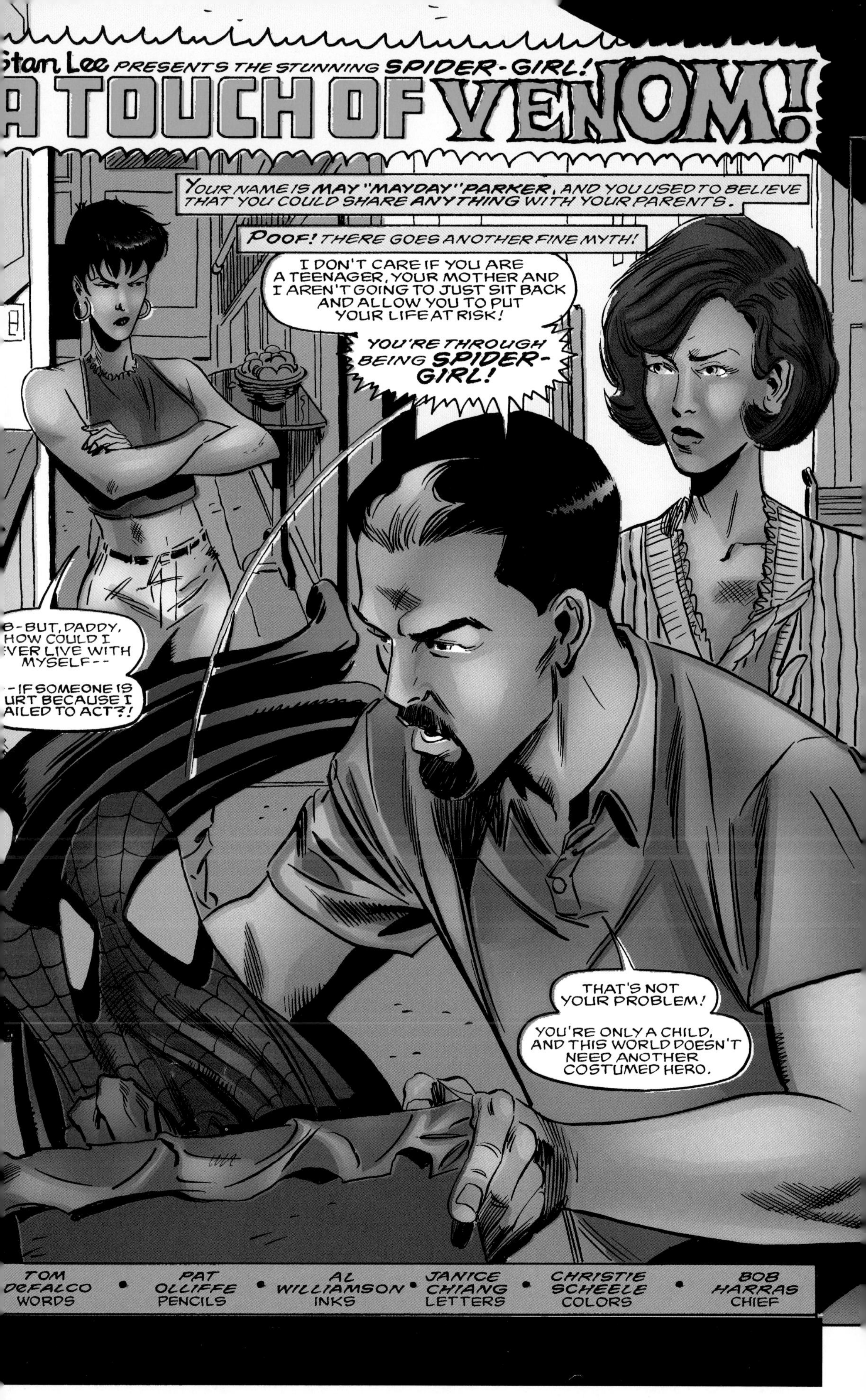
Stan Lee PRESENTS THE STUNNING SPIDER-GIRL!
A TOUCH OF VENOM!
YOUR NAME IS MAY "MAYDAY" PARKER, AND YOU USED TO BELIEVE THAT YOU COULD SHARE ANYTHING WITH YOUR PARENTS.
POOF! THERE GOES ANOTHER FINE MYTH!
I DON'T CARE IF YOU ARE A TEENAGER, YOUR MOTHER AND I AREN'T GOING TO JUST SIT BACK AND ALLOW YOU TO PUT YOUR LIFE AT RISK!
YOU'RE THROUGH BEING SPIDER-GIRL!
B-BUT, DADDY, HOW COULD I EVER LIVE WITH MYSELF--
--IF SOMEONE IS HURT BECAUSE I FAILED TO ACT?!
THAT'S NOT YOUR PROBLEM!
YOU'RE ONLY A CHILD, AND THIS WORLD DOESN'T NEED ANOTHER COSTUMED HERO.
TOM DEFALCO WORDS • PAT OLLIFFE PENCILS • AL WILLIAMSON INKS • JANICE CHIANG LETTERS • CHRISTIE SCHEELE COLORS • BOB HARRAS CHIEF

VISIT US AT

www.abdopub.com

Spotlight, a division of ABDO Publishing Company Inc., is the school and library distributor of the Marvel Entertainment books.

Library bound edition © 2006

Library of Congress Cataloging-in-Publication Data

A Touch of Venom!

ISBN 1-59961-026-4 (Reinforced Library Bound Edition)

All Spotlight books are reinforced library binding
and manufactured in the United States of America

Spotlight

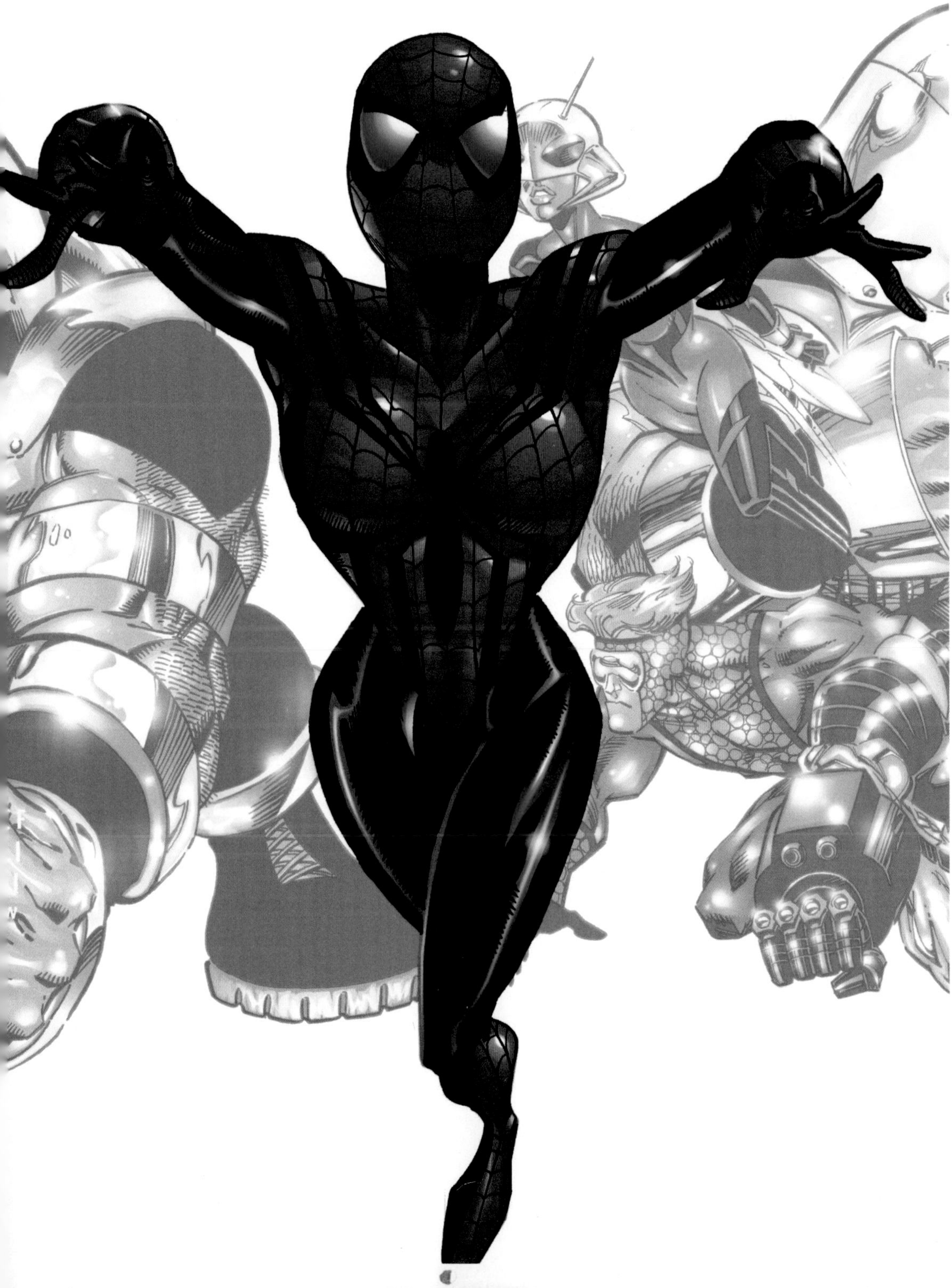

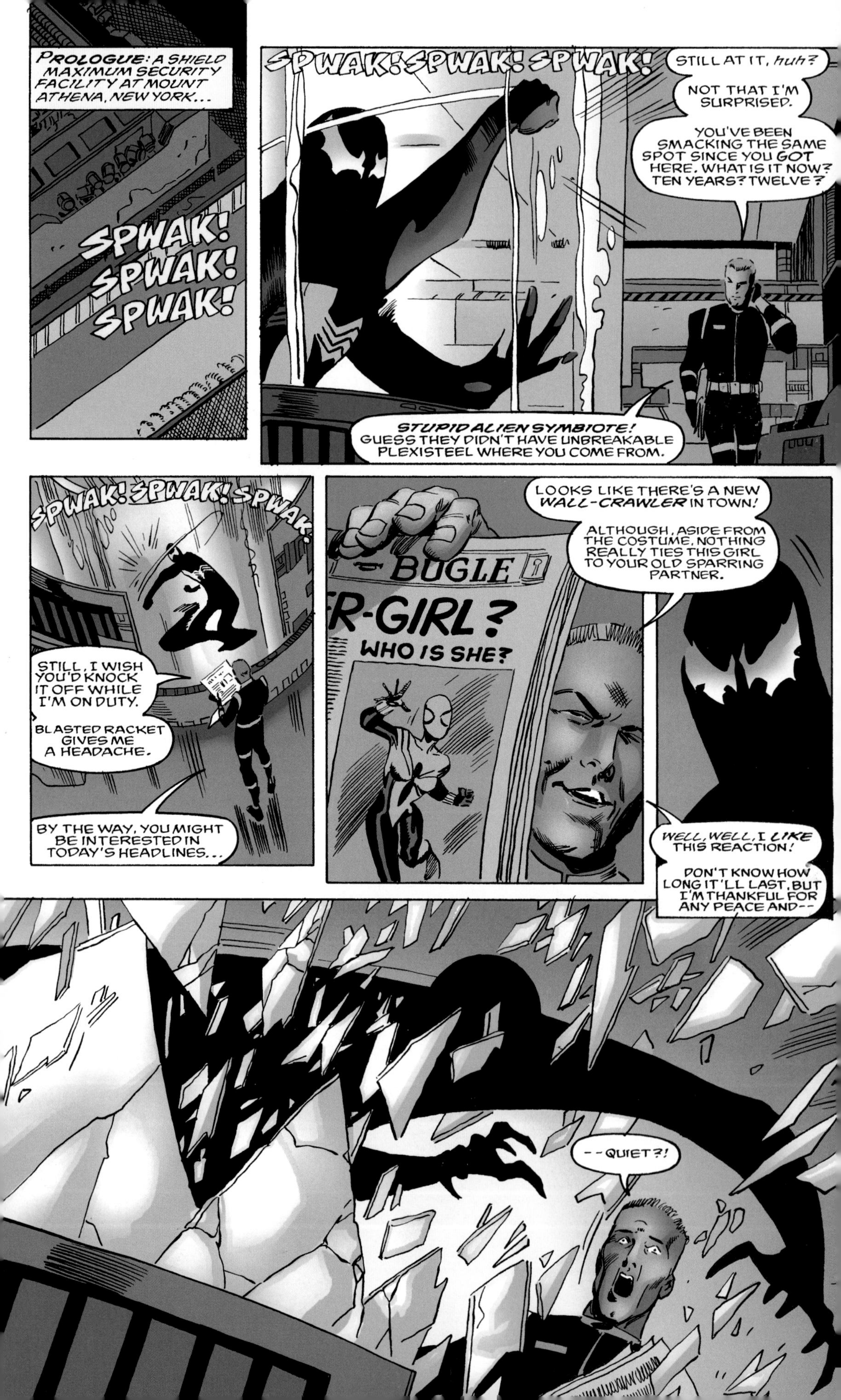
PROLOGUE: A SHIELD MAXIMUM SECURITY FACILITY AT MOUNT ATHENA, NEW YORK...
SPWAK! SPWAK! SPWAK!
SPWAK! SPWAK! SPWAK!
STILL AT IT, huh?
NOT THAT I'M SURPRISED.
YOU'VE BEEN SMACKING THE SAME SPOT SINCE YOU GOT HERE. WHAT IS IT NOW? TEN YEARS? TWELVE?
STUPID ALIEN SYMBIOTE! GUESS THEY DIDN'T HAVE UNBREAKABLE PLEXISTEEL WHERE YOU COME FROM.
SPWAK! SPWAK! SPWAK!
STILL, I WISH YOU'D KNOCK IT OFF WHILE I'M ON DUTY.
BLASTED RACKET GIVES ME A HEADACHE.
BY THE WAY, YOU MIGHT BE INTERESTED IN TODAY'S HEADLINES...
BUGLE
R-GIRL?
WHO IS SHE?
LOOKS LIKE THERE'S A NEW WALL-CRAWLER IN TOWN!
ALTHOUGH, ASIDE FROM THE COSTUME, NOTHING REALLY TIES THIS GIRL TO YOUR OLD SPARRING PARTNER.
WELL, WELL, I LIKE THIS REACTION!
DON'T KNOW HOW LONG IT'LL LAST, BUT I'M THANKFUL FOR ANY PEACE AND--
--QUIET?!

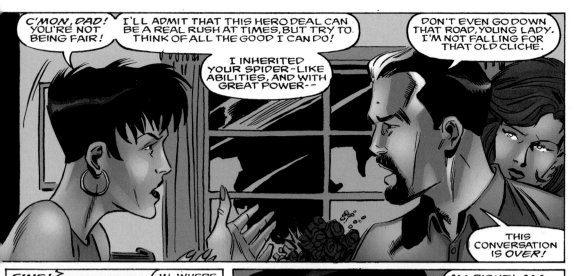

C'MON, DAD! YOU'RE NOT BEING FAIR!

I'LL ADMIT THAT THIS HERO DEAL CAN BE A REAL RUSH AT TIMES, BUT TRY TO THINK OF ALL THE GOOD I CAN DO!

I INHERITED YOUR SPIDER-LIKE ABILITIES, AND WITH GREAT POWER--

DON'T EVEN GO DOWN THAT ROAD, YOUNG LADY. I'M NOT FALLING FOR THAT OLD CLICHE.

THIS CONVERSATION IS OVER!

FINE! YOU WIN!

W-WHERE ARE YOU GOING, MAY?

OUT!

THAT'S NOT HOW YOU ANSWER YOUR MOTHER!

ALL RIGHT! ALL RIGHT! I'M OFF TO BASKETBALL PRACTICE...UNLESS THAT'S ALSO FORBIDDEN!

HAPPY NOW?!

SLAM!

ECSTATIC!

YOU THINK SHE HEARD US?

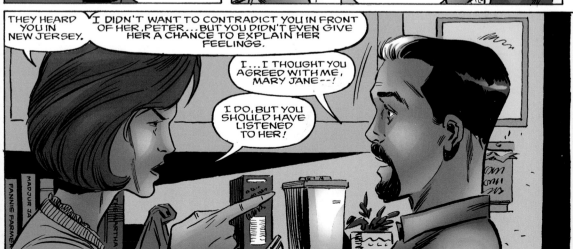

THEY HEARD YOU IN NEW JERSEY.

I DIDN'T WANT TO CONTRADICT YOU IN FRONT OF HER, PETER...BUT YOU DIDN'T EVEN GIVE HER A CHANCE TO EXPLAIN HER FEELINGS.

I...I THOUGHT YOU AGREED WITH ME, MARY JANE--!

I DO, BUT YOU SHOULD HAVE LISTENED TO HER!

FUN'N'GAMES, HUH?

ONLY A FEW WEEKS AGO, YOU WERE AN AVERAGE ALL-AMERICAN TEENAGER.

(OKAY, MAYBE AVERAGE IS STRETCHING IT FOR A GIRL WHO'S A STRAIGHT-A STUDENT, AND A STARTER FOR THE MIDTOWN HIGH GIRLS' BASKETBALL TEAM.)

ANYWAY, THAT'S WHEN YOU FIRST LEARNED ABOUT YOUR DAD'S SECRET LIFE.

HE USED TO BE THE ORIGINAL SPIDER-MAN...

(UNTIL A BATTLE WITH A SUPER-VILLAIN RESULTED IN THE LOSS OF HIS RIGHT LEG.)

HAVING RECENTLY DISCOVERED THAT YOU ALSO HAD SPIDER-LIKE POWERS, YOU ATTEMPTED TO CONTINUE THE FAMILY TRADITION.

BUT YOUR PARENTS AREN'T PLEASED.

IN FACT, YOUR ONLY SUPPORTER IS YOUR UNCLE PHIL--

--WHO, SURPRISE, SURPRISE, WAS ONCE THE COSTUMED HERO KNOWN AS THE GREEN GOBLIN!

¡Sheesh!- Is it any wonder you're so drawn to the spandex life?!

YOU'RE AT A CROSSROAD MISS PARKER...

DO YOU OBEY YOUR PARENTS, AND HANG UP YOUR WEBS LIKE A GOOD LITTLE GIRL?

OR--?!

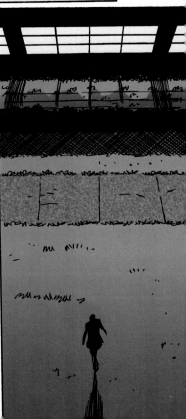

I...I CAN'T BELIEVE YOU'D EVEN CONSIDER ALLOWING MAY TO CONTINUE THIS MADNESS.

YOU'RE MISSING THE POINT, PETER.

I *HATE* THE VERY IDEA OF IT!

JUST LIKE I HATED IT WHEN YOU WERE SPIDER-MAN!

BUT I CAN UNDERSTAND HER DESIRE TO USE HER POWERS TO HELP AND PROTECT THOSE WHO MIGHT NEED A FRIENDLY NEIGHBORHOOD SUPER HERO.

WE RAISED HER TO HAVE A GOOD SENSE OF RESPONSIBILITY--

--SO WE SHOULDN'T BE SURPRISED THAT SHE WANTS TO EXERCISE IT!

B-BUT, THE DANGER--!

YOU MIGHT BE ABLE TO LESSEN IT... BY GIVING HER THE BENEFIT OF YOUR EXPERIENCE.

I KNOW SHE'S ALMOST A GROWN WOMAN, BUT MAY DOESN'T UNDERSTAND THE TRUE COSTS OF PLAYING HERO.

I'M MISSING A LEG... BECAUSE I WAS OUT RISKING MY NECK... WHEN I SHOULD HAVE BEEN PROVIDING FOR MY FAMILY.

I HAVE A RESPONSIBILITY TO PROTECT HER FROM SUFFERING THE SAME FATE OR WORSE!

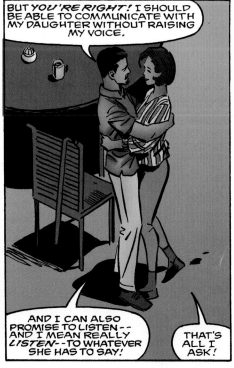

BUT *YOU'RE RIGHT!* I SHOULD BE ABLE TO COMMUNICATE WITH MY DAUGHTER WITHOUT RAISING MY VOICE.

AND I CAN ALSO PROMISE TO LISTEN-- AND I MEAN REALLY *LISTEN*--TO WHATEVER SHE HAS TO SAY!

THAT'S ALL I ASK!

IF IT'S OKAY WITH YOU, I'LL CATCH THE END OF HER PRACTICE, AND TAKE HER FOR A SODA OR SOMETHING.

SOUNDS LIKE A PLAN.

YOU TWO NEED SOME QUALITY TIME.

HE WALKS SLOWLY--

--LOST IN THOUGHTS OF HIS OWN ADVENTUROUS YOUTH.

HE TRIES TO REMEMBER CLOSE CALLS, RECKLESS CHANCES, AND DESPERATE SITUATIONS.

BUT HIS ONLY CLEAR RECOLLECTION IS THE COOL SNAP OF THE WIND AS HE SWUNG-- UPSIDE-DOWN-- ON SLENDER STRANDS OF WEBBING.

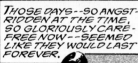

THOSE DAYS--SO ANGST- RIDDEN AT THE TIME, SO GLORIOUSLY CARE- FREE NOW--SEEMED LIKE THEY WOULD LAST FOREVER.

BUT HIS TIME AS A COSTUMED ADVENTURER ENDED ALL TOO SUDDENLY.

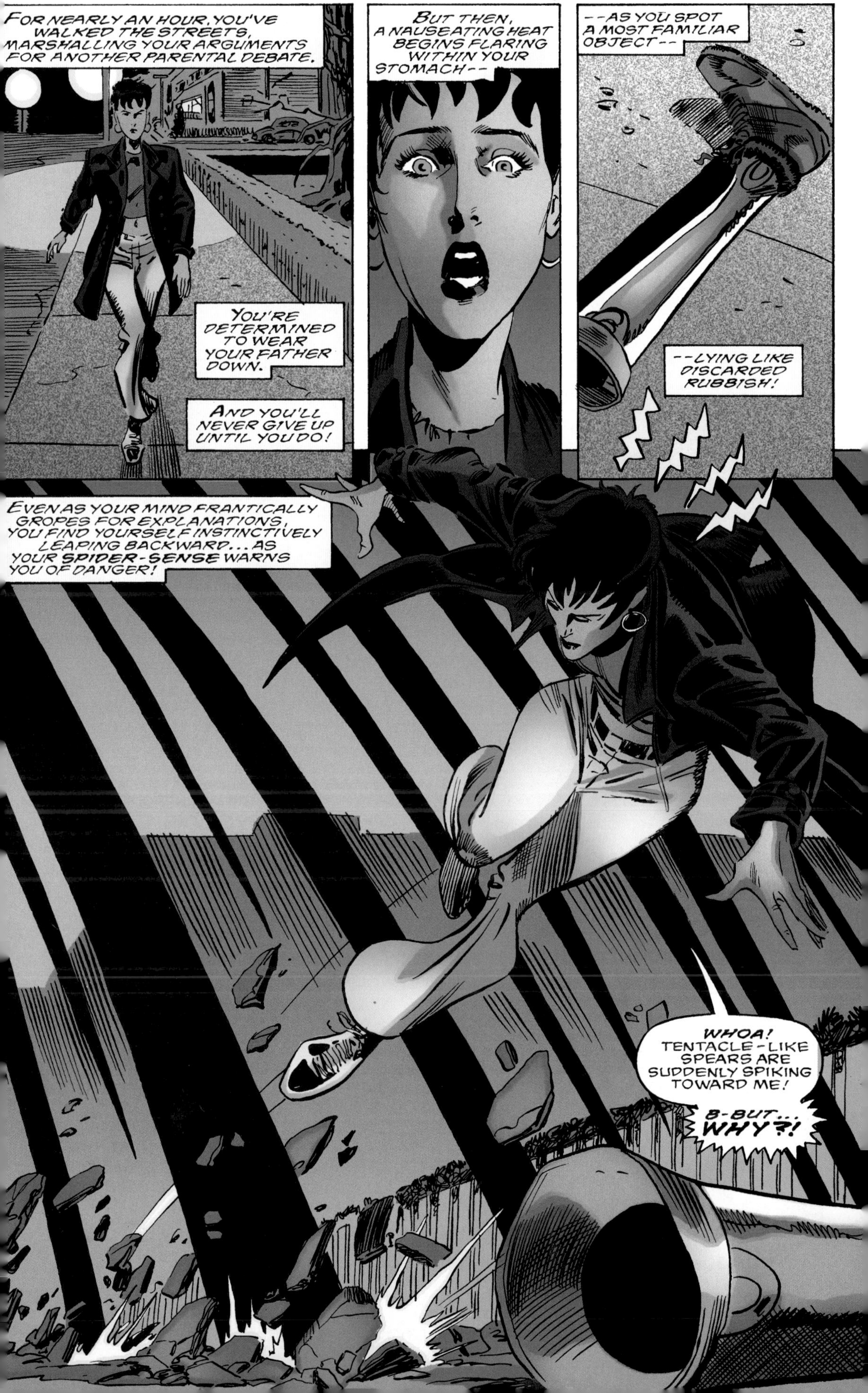
FOR NEARLY AN HOUR, YOU'VE WALKED THE STREETS, MARSHALLING YOUR ARGUMENTS FOR ANOTHER PARENTAL DEBATE.
YOU'RE DETERMINED TO WEAR YOUR FATHER DOWN.
AND YOU'LL NEVER GIVE UP UNTIL YOU DO!
BUT THEN, A NAUSEATING HEAT BEGINS FLARING WITHIN YOUR STOMACH--
--AS YOU SPOT A MOST FAMILIAR OBJECT--
--LYING LIKE DISCARDED RUBBISH!
EVEN AS YOUR MIND FRANTICALLY GROPES FOR EXPLANATIONS, YOU FIND YOURSELF INSTINCTIVELY LEAPING BACKWARD... AS YOUR SPIDER-SENSE WARNS YOU OF DANGER!
WHOA! TENTACLE-LIKE SPEARS ARE SUDDENLY SPIKING TOWARD ME!
B-BUT... WHY?!

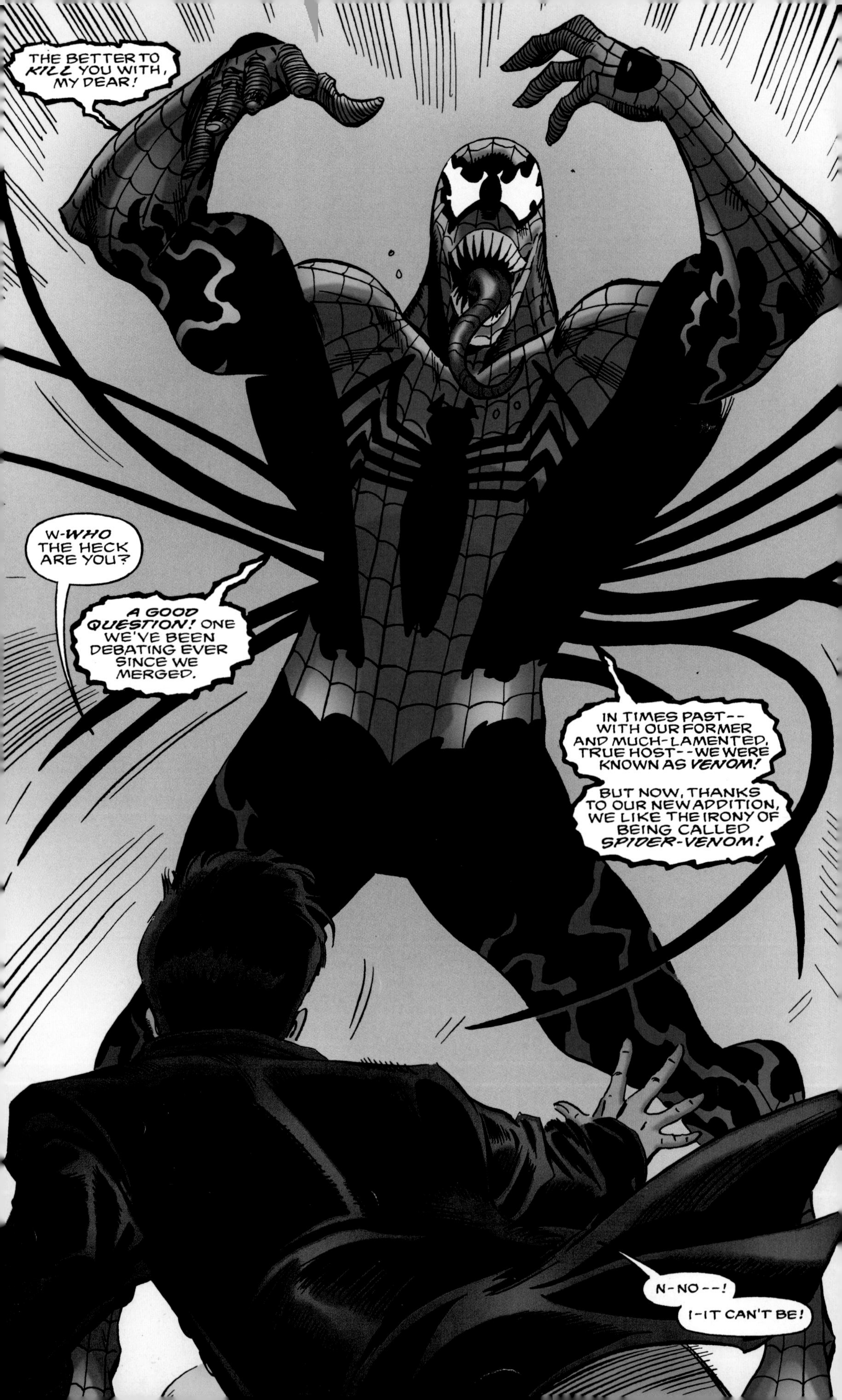
THE BETTER TO KILL YOU WITH, MY DEAR!
W-WHO THE HECK ARE YOU?
A GOOD QUESTION! ONE WE'VE BEEN DEBATING EVER SINCE WE MERGED.
IN TIMES PAST-- WITH OUR FORMER AND MUCH-LAMENTED, TRUE HOST--WE WERE KNOWN AS VENOM!
BUT NOW, THANKS TO OUR NEW ADDITION, WE LIKE THE IRONY OF BEING CALLED SPIDER-VENOM!
N-NO--!
I-IT CAN'T BE!

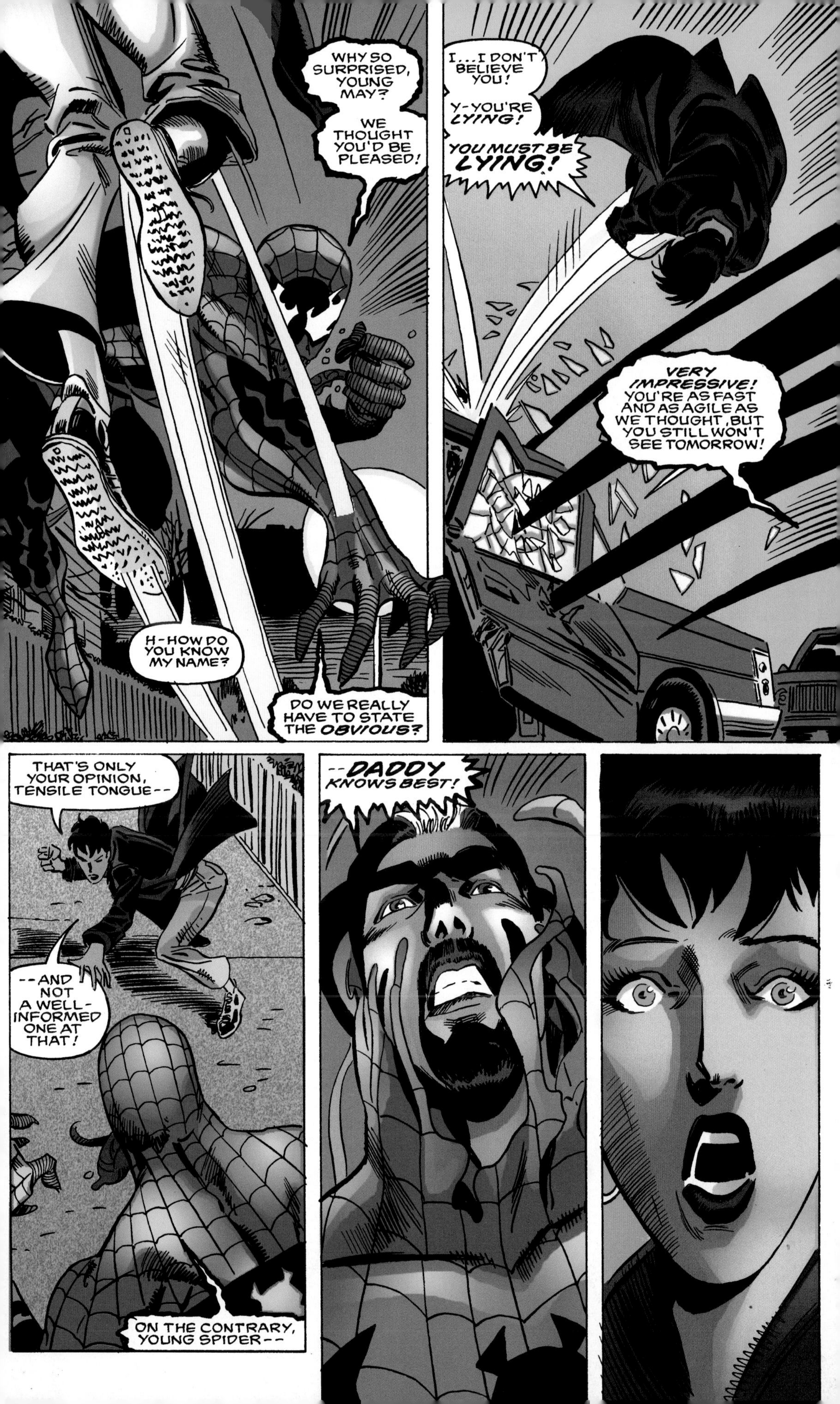

WHY SO SURPRISED, YOUNG MAY?
WE THOUGHT YOU'D BE PLEASED!
H-HOW DO YOU KNOW MY NAME?
DO WE REALLY HAVE TO STATE THE OBVIOUS?
I...I DON'T BELIEVE YOU!
Y-YOU'RE LYING!
YOU MUST BE LYING!
VERY IMPRESSIVE! YOU'RE AS FAST AND AS AGILE AS WE THOUGHT, BUT YOU STILL WON'T SEE TOMORROW!
THAT'S ONLY YOUR OPINION, TENSILE TONGUE--
--AND NOT A WELL-INFORMED ONE AT THAT!
ON THE CONTRARY, YOUNG SPIDER--
--DADDY KNOWS BEST!

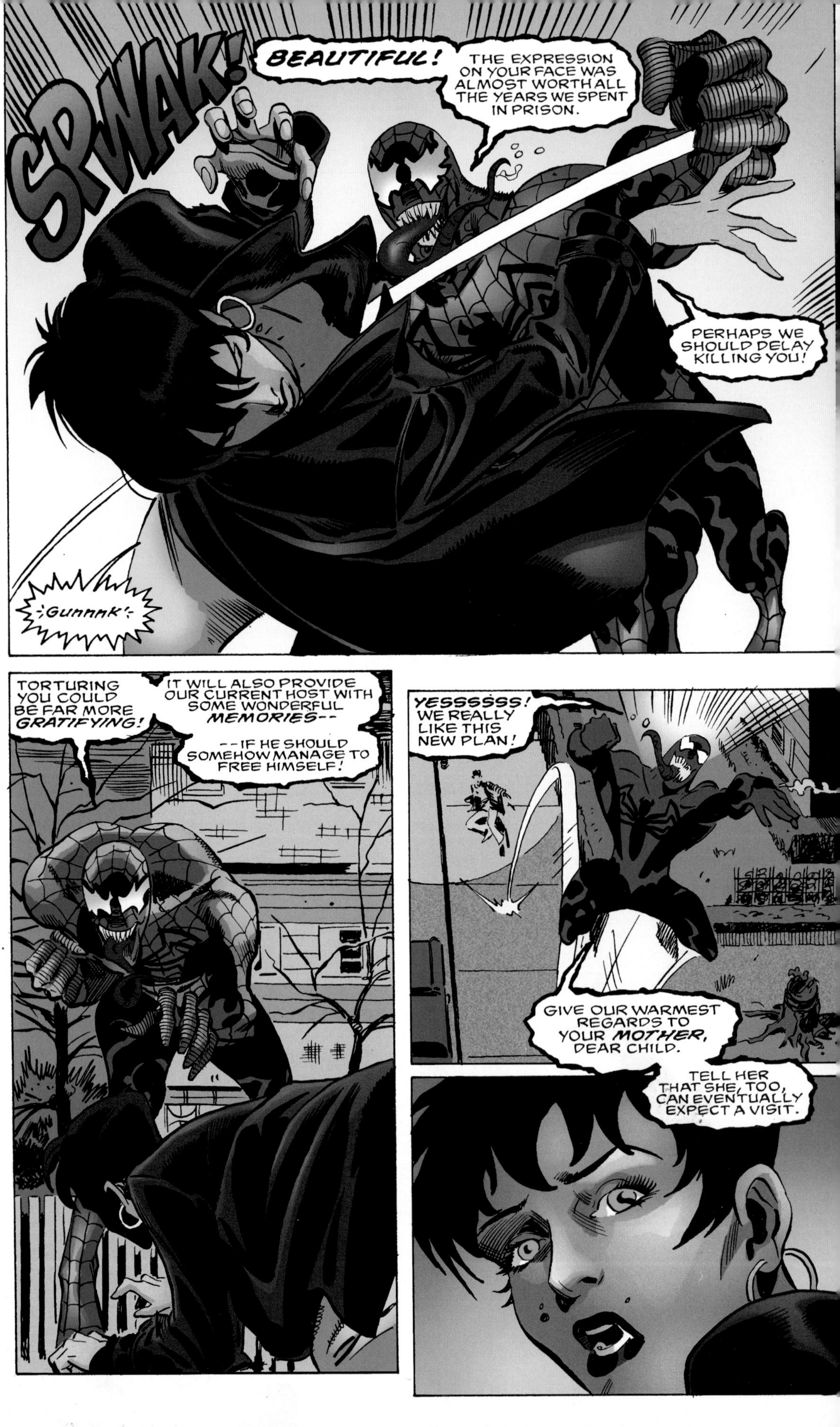
SPWAK!
BEAUTIFUL!
THE EXPRESSION ON YOUR FACE WAS ALMOST WORTH ALL THE YEARS WE SPENT IN PRISON.
PERHAPS WE SHOULD DELAY KILLING YOU!
Gunnnk
TORTURING YOU COULD BE FAR MORE GRATIFYING!
IT WILL ALSO PROVIDE OUR CURRENT HOST WITH SOME WONDERFUL MEMORIES--
--IF HE SHOULD SOMEHOW MANAGE TO FREE HIMSELF!
YESSSSSS! WE REALLY LIKE THIS NEW PLAN!
GIVE OUR WARMEST REGARDS TO YOUR MOTHER, DEAR CHILD.
TELL HER THAT SHE, TOO, CAN EVENTUALLY EXPECT A VISIT.

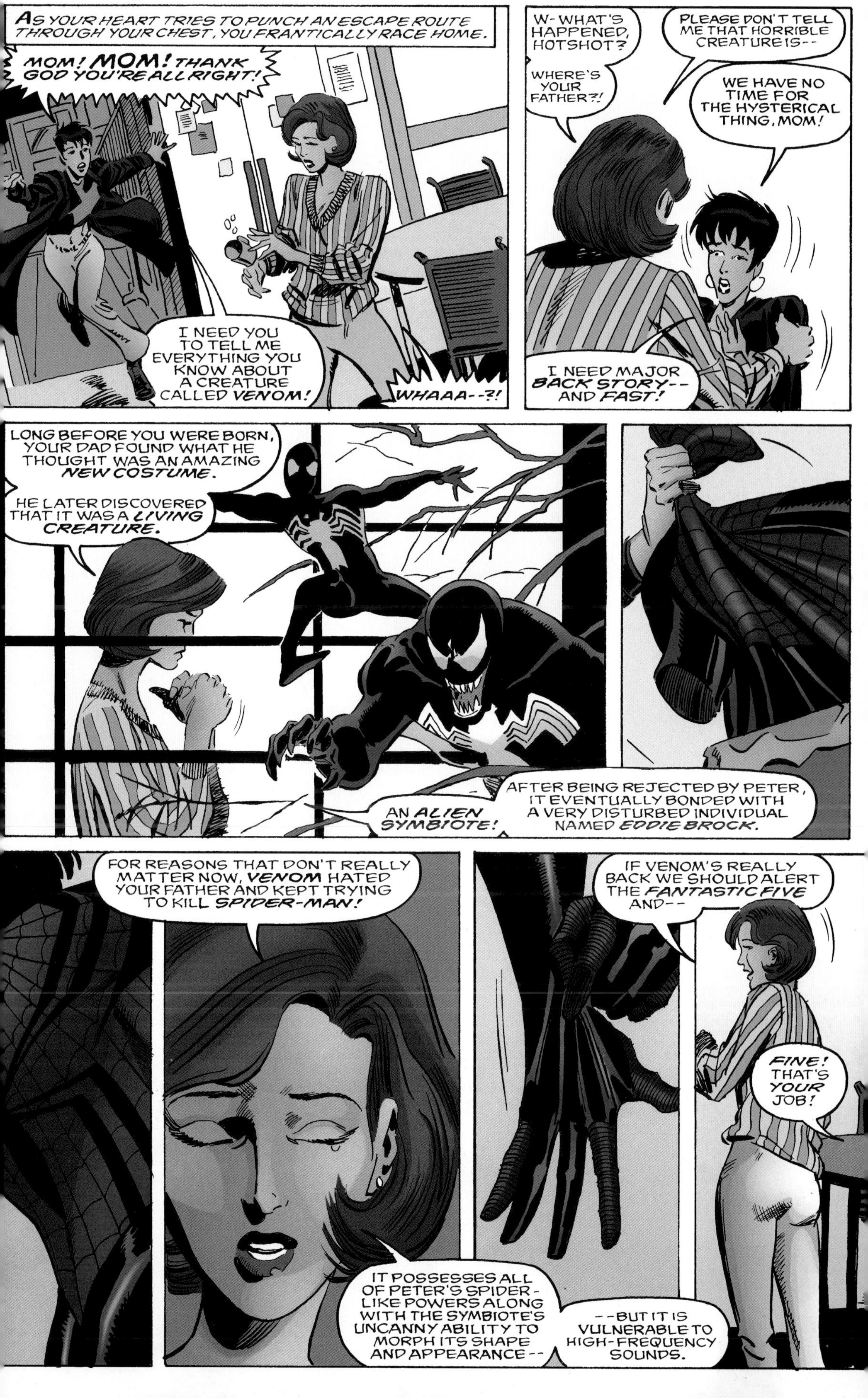
AS YOUR HEART TRIES TO PUNCH AN ESCAPE ROUTE THROUGH YOUR CHEST, YOU FRANTICALLY RACE HOME.
MOM! MOM! THANK GOD YOU'RE ALL RIGHT!
I NEED YOU TO TELL ME EVERYTHING YOU KNOW ABOUT A CREATURE CALLED VENOM!
WHAAA--?!
W-WHAT'S HAPPENED, HOTSHOT?
WHERE'S YOUR FATHER?!
PLEASE DON'T TELL ME THAT HORRIBLE CREATURE IS--
WE HAVE NO TIME FOR THE HYSTERICAL THING, MOM!
I NEED MAJOR BACK STORY-- AND FAST!
LONG BEFORE YOU WERE BORN, YOUR DAD FOUND WHAT HE THOUGHT WAS AN AMAZING NEW COSTUME.
HE LATER DISCOVERED THAT IT WAS A LIVING CREATURE.
AN ALIEN SYMBIOTE!
AFTER BEING REJECTED BY PETER, IT EVENTUALLY BONDED WITH A VERY DISTURBED INDIVIDUAL NAMED EDDIE BROCK.
FOR REASONS THAT DON'T REALLY MATTER NOW, VENOM HATED YOUR FATHER AND KEPT TRYING TO KILL SPIDER-MAN!
IF VENOM'S REALLY BACK WE SHOULD ALERT THE FANTASTIC FIVE AND--
FINE! THAT'S YOUR JOB!
IT POSSESSES ALL OF PETER'S SPIDER-LIKE POWERS ALONG WITH THE SYMBIOTE'S UNCANNY ABILITY TO MORPH ITS SHAPE AND APPEARANCE--
--BUT IT IS VULNERABLE TO HIGH-FREQUENCY SOUNDS.

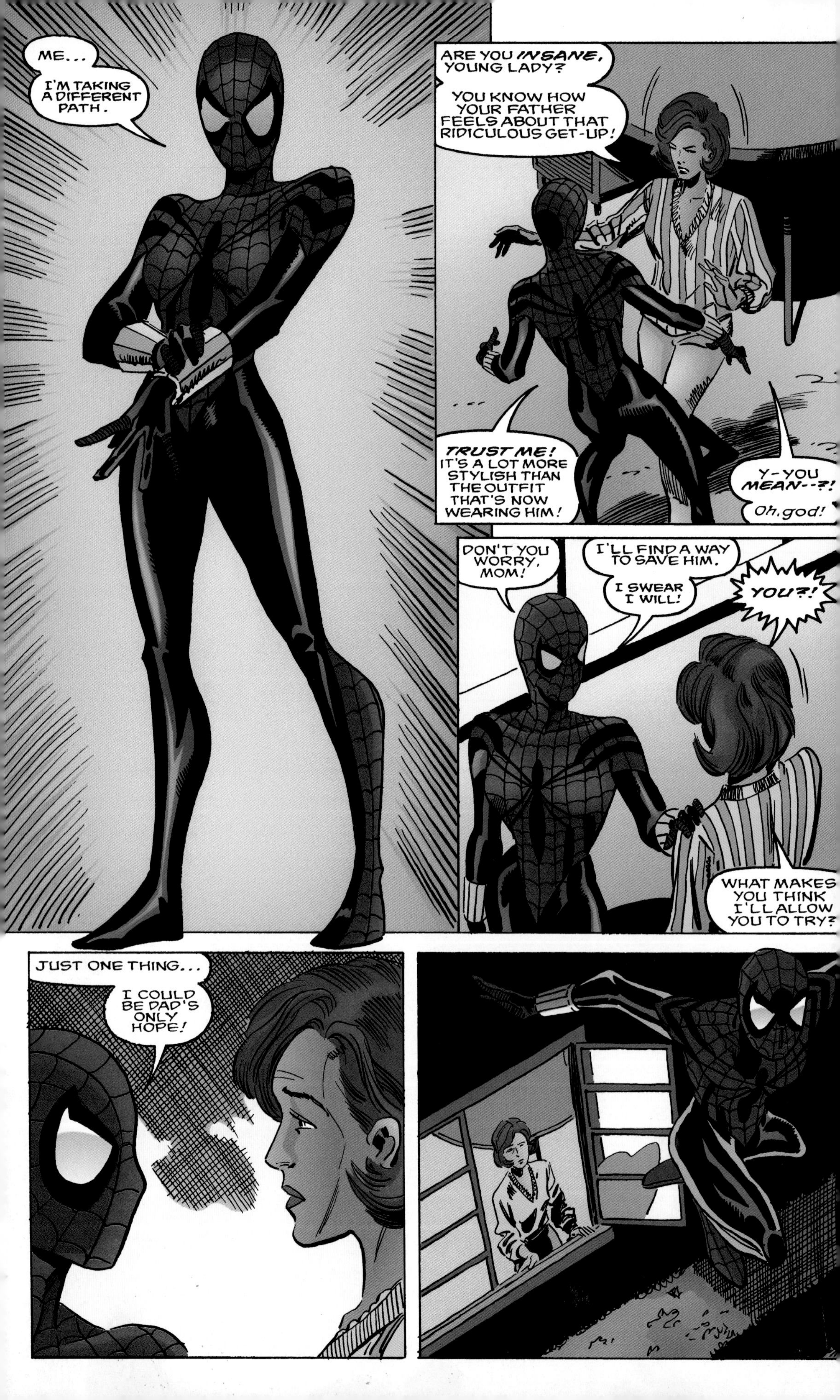

ME...
I'M TAKING A DIFFERENT PATH.
ARE YOU INSANE, YOUNG LADY?
YOU KNOW HOW YOUR FATHER FEELS ABOUT THAT RIDICULOUS GET-UP!
TRUST ME! IT'S A LOT MORE STYLISH THAN THE OUTFIT THAT'S NOW WEARING HIM!
Y-YOU MEAN--?!
Oh, god!
DON'T YOU WORRY, MOM!
I'LL FIND A WAY TO SAVE HIM.
I SWEAR I WILL!
YOU?!
WHAT MAKES YOU THINK I'LL ALLOW YOU TO TRY?
JUST ONE THING...
I COULD BE DAD'S ONLY HOPE!

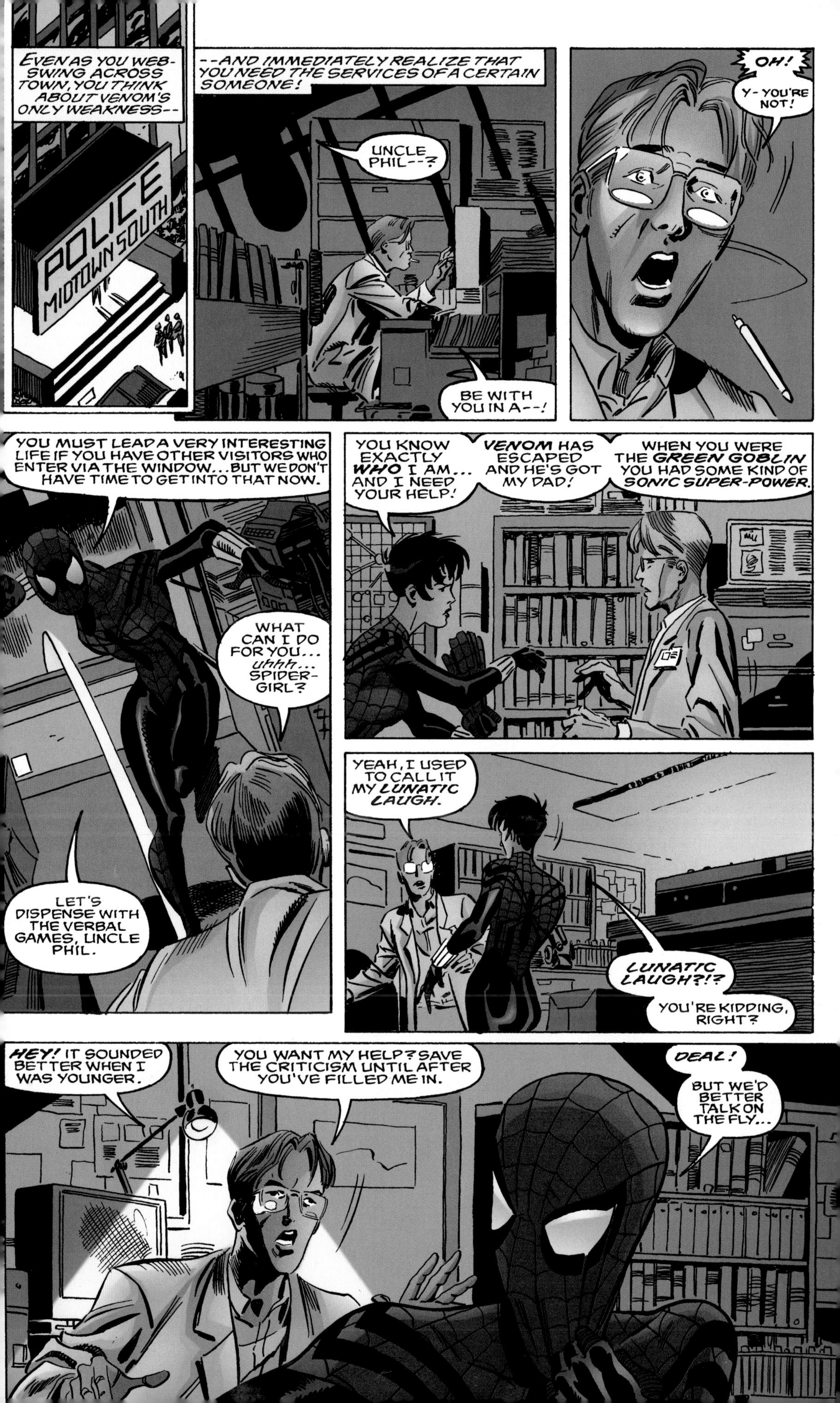
EVEN AS YOU WEB-SWING ACROSS TOWN, YOU THINK ABOUT VENOM'S ONLY WEAKNESS--
POLICE
MIDTOWN SOUTH
--AND IMMEDIATELY REALIZE THAT YOU NEED THE SERVICES OF A CERTAIN SOMEONE!
UNCLE PHIL--?
BE WITH YOU IN A--!
OH!
Y-YOU'RE NOT!
YOU MUST LEAD A VERY INTERESTING LIFE IF YOU HAVE OTHER VISITORS WHO ENTER VIA THE WINDOW... BUT WE DON'T HAVE TIME TO GET INTO THAT NOW.
WHAT CAN I DO FOR YOU... uhhh... SPIDER-GIRL?
LET'S DISPENSE WITH THE VERBAL GAMES, UNCLE PHIL.
YOU KNOW EXACTLY WHO I AM... AND I NEED YOUR HELP!
VENOM HAS ESCAPED AND HE'S GOT MY DAD!
WHEN YOU WERE THE GREEN GOBLIN YOU HAD SOME KIND OF SONIC SUPER-POWER.
YEAH, I USED TO CALL IT MY LUNATIC LAUGH.
LUNATIC LAUGH?!?
YOU'RE KIDDING, RIGHT?
HEY! IT SOUNDED BETTER WHEN I WAS YOUNGER.
YOU WANT MY HELP? SAVE THE CRITICISM UNTIL AFTER YOU'VE FILLED ME IN.
DEAL!
BUT WE'D BETTER TALK ON THE FLY...

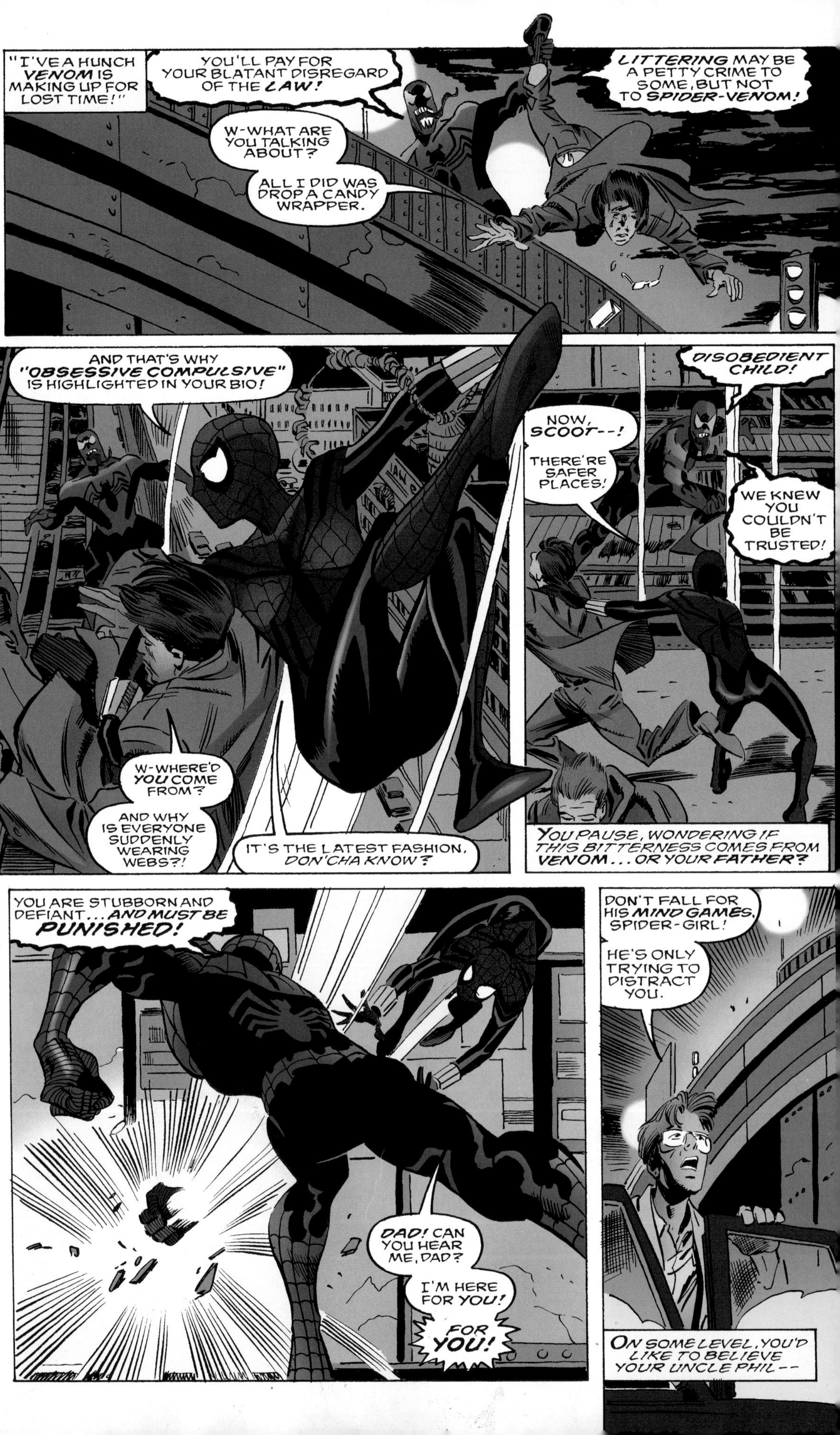

"I'VE A HUNCH VENOM IS MAKING UP FOR LOST TIME!"
YOU'LL PAY FOR YOUR BLATANT DISREGARD OF THE LAW!
W-WHAT ARE YOU TALKING ABOUT?
ALL I DID WAS DROP A CANDY WRAPPER.
LITTERING MAY BE A PETTY CRIME TO SOME, BUT NOT TO SPIDER-VENOM!
AND THAT'S WHY "OBSESSIVE COMPULSIVE" IS HIGHLIGHTED IN YOUR BIO!
W-WHERE'D YOU COME FROM?
AND WHY IS EVERYONE SUDDENLY WEARING WEBS?!
IT'S THE LATEST FASHION, DON'CHA KNOW?
DISOBEDIENT CHILD!
NOW, SCOOT--!
THERE'RE SAFER PLACES!
WE KNEW YOU COULDN'T BE TRUSTED!
YOU PAUSE, WONDERING IF THIS BITTERNESS COMES FROM VENOM... OR YOUR FATHER?
YOU ARE STUBBORN AND DEFIANT... AND MUST BE PUNISHED!
DAD! CAN YOU HEAR ME, DAD?
I'M HERE FOR YOU!
FOR YOU!
DON'T FALL FOR HIS MIND GAMES, SPIDER-GIRL!
HE'S ONLY TRYING TO DISTRACT YOU.
ON SOME LEVEL, YOU'D LIKE TO BELIEVE YOUR UNCLE PHIL--

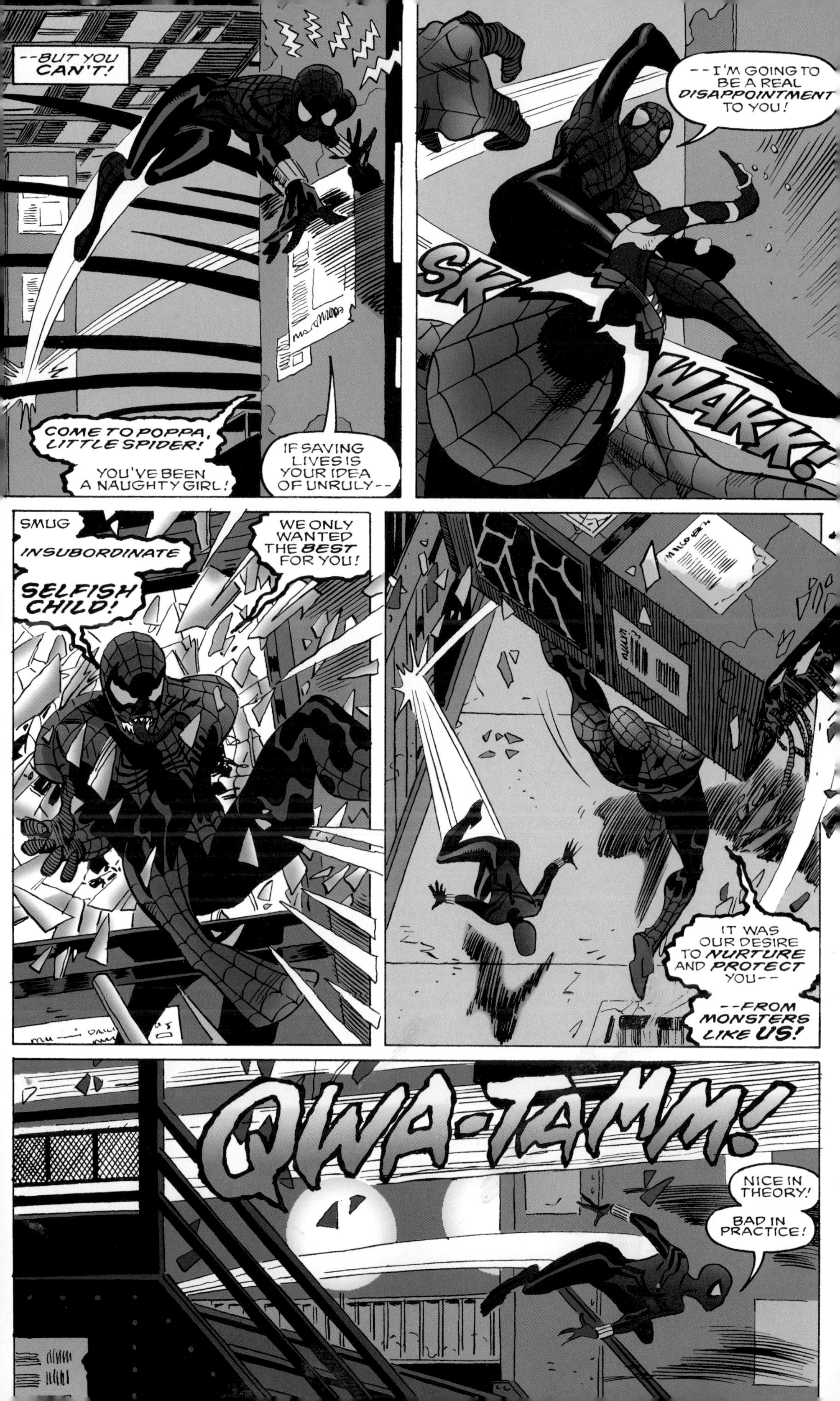
--BUT YOU CAN'T!
COME TO POPPA, LITTLE SPIDER!
YOU'VE BEEN A NAUGHTY GIRL!
IF SAVING LIVES IS YOUR IDEA OF UNRULY--
--I'M GOING TO BE A REAL DISAPPOINTMENT TO YOU!
SKWAKK!
SMUG
INSUBORDINATE
SELFISH CHILD!
WE ONLY WANTED THE BEST FOR YOU!
IT WAS OUR DESIRE TO NURTURE AND PROTECT YOU--
--FROM MONSTERS LIKE US!
QWA-TAMM!
NICE IN THEORY!
BAD IN PRACTICE!

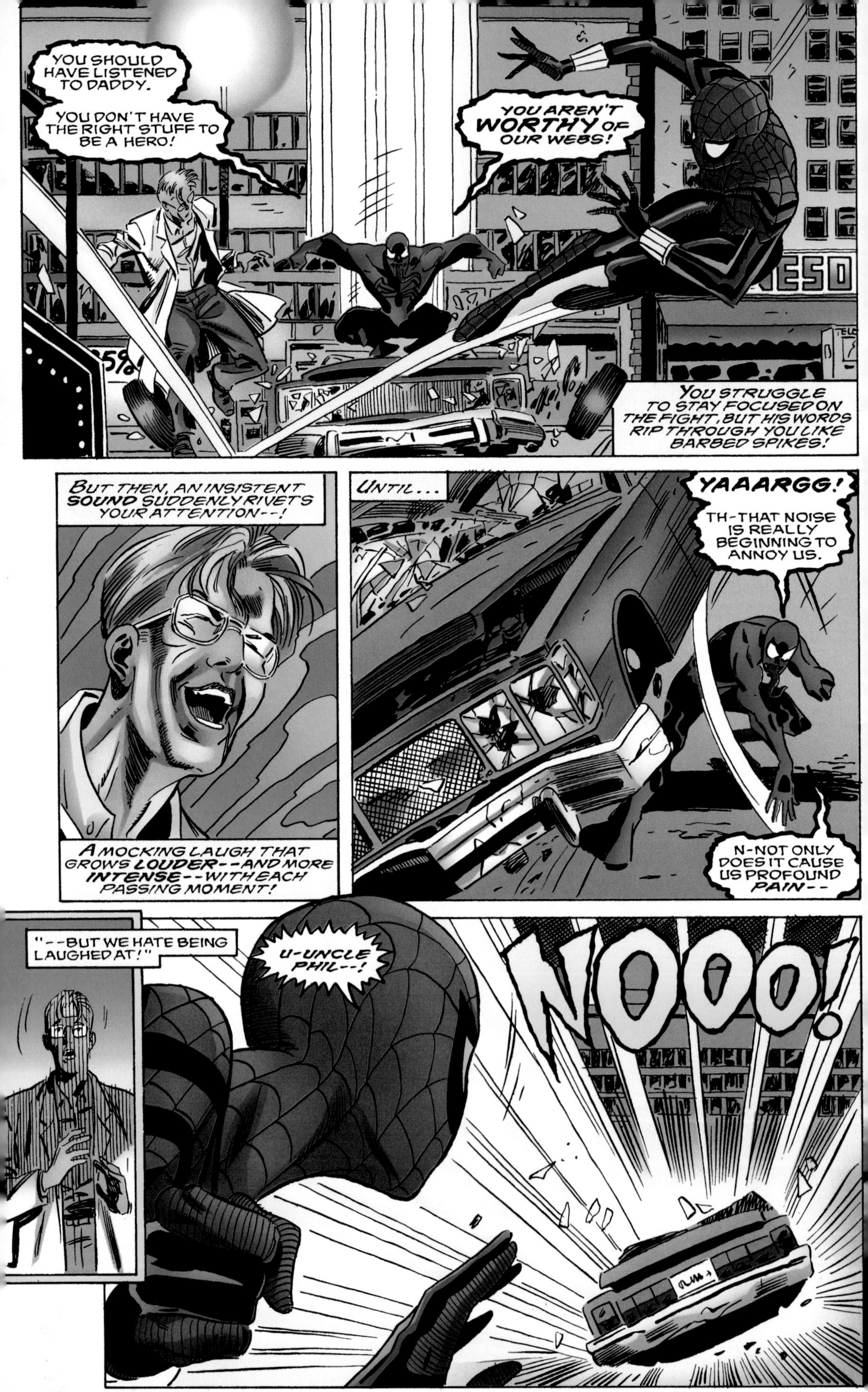
YOU SHOULD HAVE LISTENED TO DADDY.
YOU DON'T HAVE THE RIGHT STUFF TO BE A HERO!
YOU AREN'T WORTHY OF OUR WEBS!
YOU STRUGGLE TO STAY FOCUSED ON THE FIGHT, BUT HIS WORDS RIP THROUGH YOU LIKE BARBED SPIKES!
BUT THEN, AN INSISTENT SOUND SUDDENLY RIVETS YOUR ATTENTION--!
A MOCKING LAUGH THAT GROWS LOUDER--AND MORE INTENSE--WITH EACH PASSING MOMENT!
UNTIL...
YAAARGG!
TH-THAT NOISE IS REALLY BEGINNING TO ANNOY US.
N-NOT ONLY DOES IT CAUSE US PROFOUND PAIN--
"--BUT WE HATE BEING LAUGHED AT!"
U-UNCLE PHIL--!
NOOO!

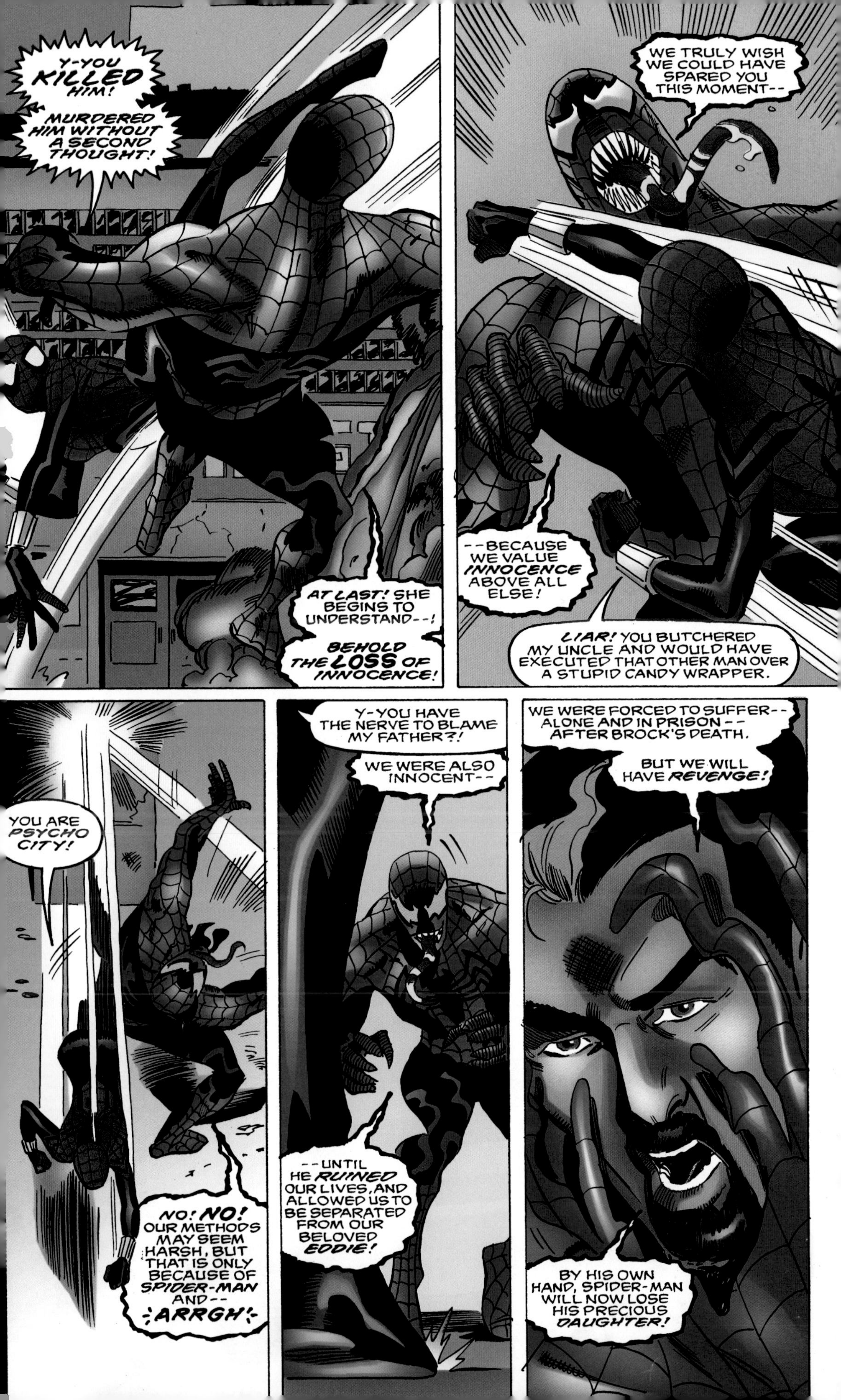
Y-YOU KILLED HIM!
MURDERED HIM WITHOUT A SECOND THOUGHT!
AT LAST! SHE BEGINS TO UNDERSTAND--!
BEHOLD THE LOSS OF INNOCENCE!
WE TRULY WISH WE COULD HAVE SPARED YOU THIS MOMENT--
--BECAUSE WE VALUE INNOCENCE ABOVE ALL ELSE!
LIAR! YOU BUTCHERED MY UNCLE AND WOULD HAVE EXECUTED THAT OTHER MAN OVER A STUPID CANDY WRAPPER.
YOU ARE PSYCHO CITY!
NO! NO! OUR METHODS MAY SEEM HARSH, BUT THAT IS ONLY BECAUSE OF SPIDER-MAN AND--
ARRGH
Y-YOU HAVE THE NERVE TO BLAME MY FATHER?!
WE WERE ALSO INNOCENT--
--UNTIL HE RUINED OUR LIVES, AND ALLOWED US TO BE SEPARATED FROM OUR BELOVED EDDIE!
WE WERE FORCED TO SUFFER--ALONE AND IN PRISON--AFTER BROCK'S DEATH.
BUT WE WILL HAVE REVENGE!
BY HIS OWN HAND, SPIDER-MAN WILL NOW LOSE HIS PRECIOUS DAUGHTER!

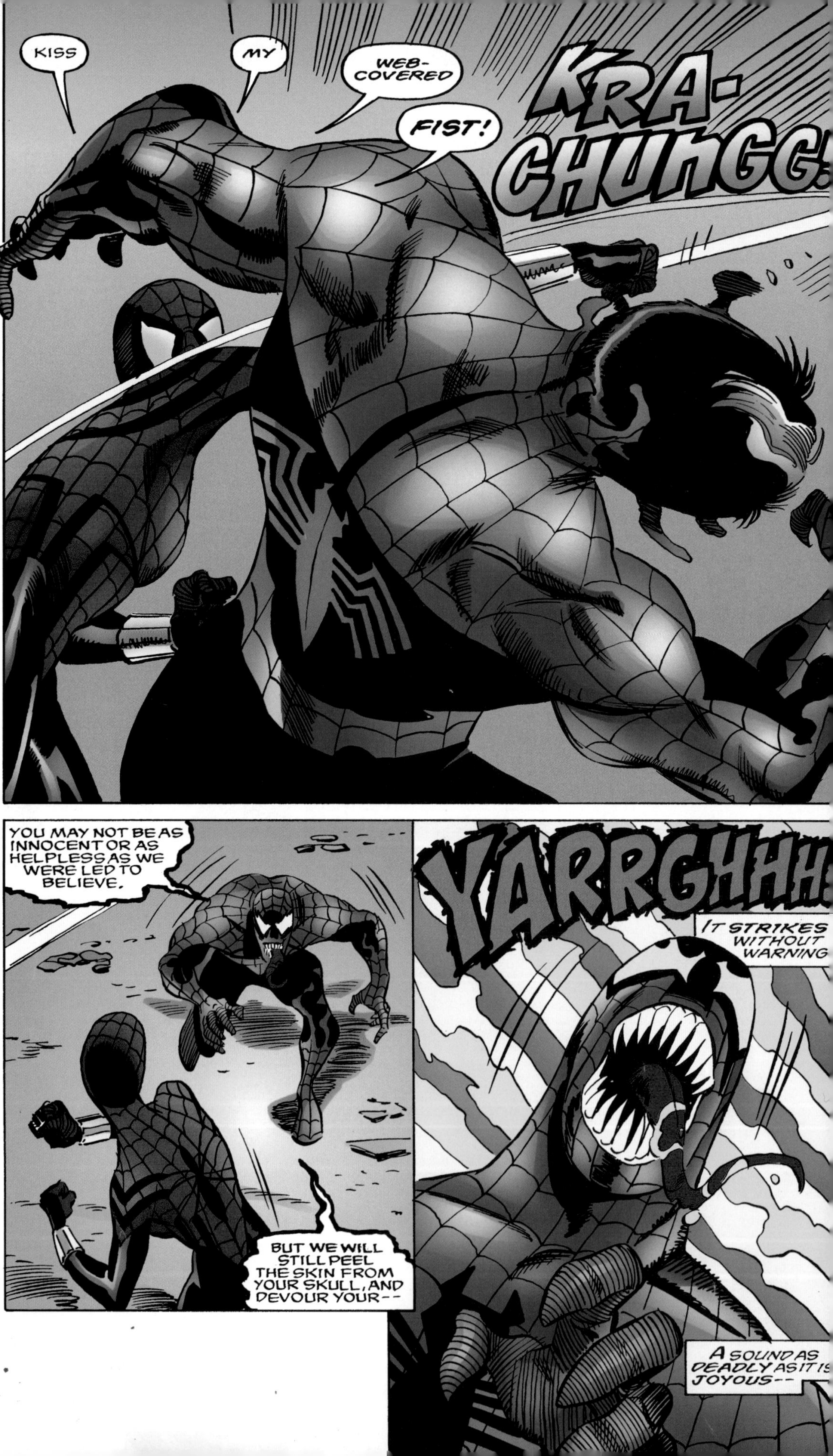

KISS
MY
WEB-COVERED
FIST!
KRA-CHUNGG
YOU MAY NOT BE AS INNOCENT OR AS HELPLESS AS WE WERE LED TO BELIEVE.
BUT WE WILL STILL PEEL THE SKIN FROM YOUR SKULL, AND DEVOUR YOUR--
YARRGHHH
IT STRIKES WITHOUT WARNING
A SOUND AS DEADLY AS IT IS JOYOUS--

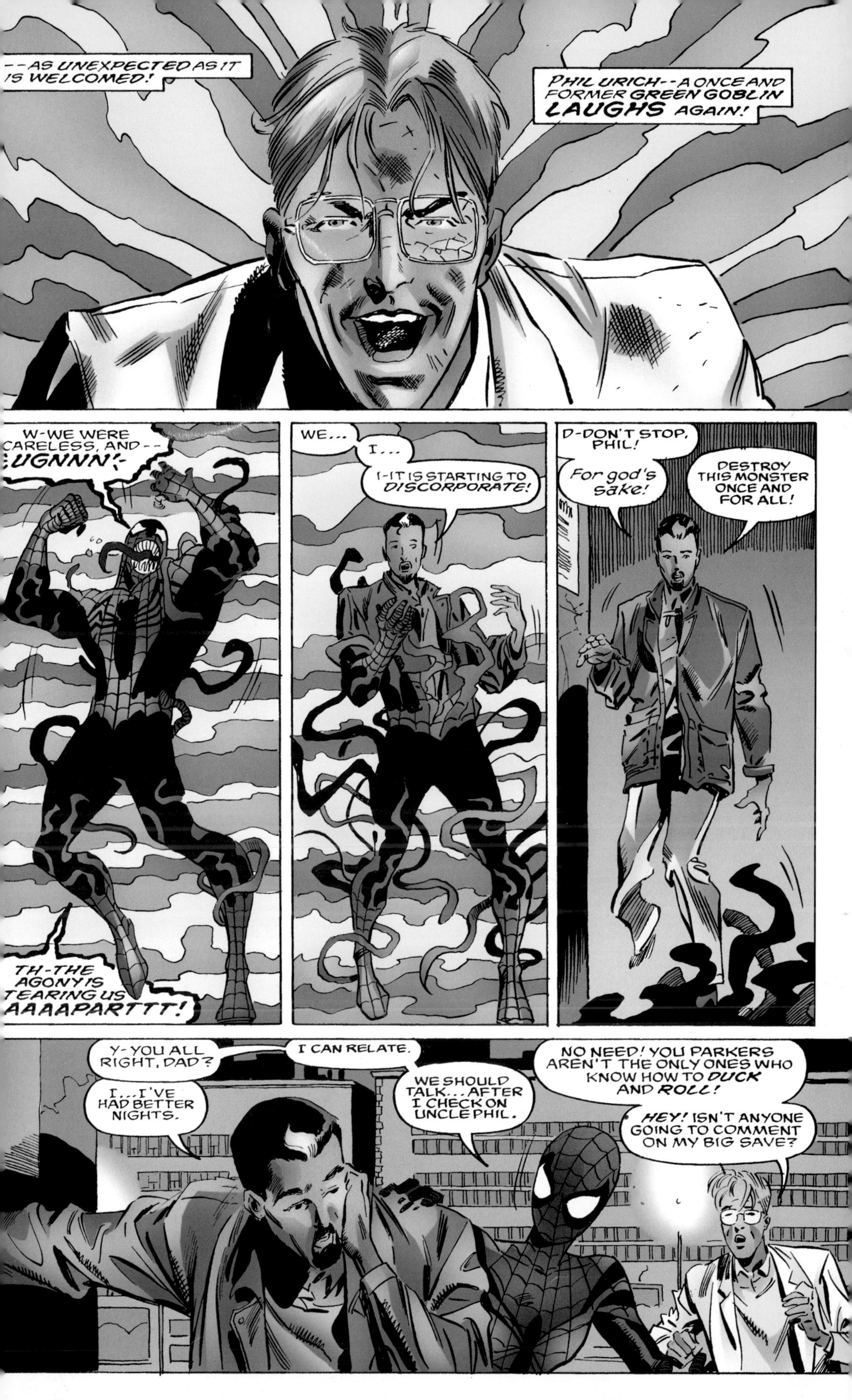
--AS UNEXPECTED AS IT IS WELCOMED!
PHIL URICH--A ONCE AND FORMER GREEN GOBLIN LAUGHS AGAIN!
W-WE WERE CARELESS, AND--EUGNNN!
TH-THE AGONY IS TEARING US AAAAPARTTTT!
WE...
I...
I-IT IS STARTING TO DISCORPORATE!
D-DON'T STOP, PHIL!
For god's sake!
DESTROY THIS MONSTER ONCE AND FOR ALL!
Y-YOU ALL RIGHT, DAD?
I...I'VE HAD BETTER NIGHTS.
I CAN RELATE.
WE SHOULD TALK...AFTER I CHECK ON UNCLE PHIL.
NO NEED! YOU PARKERS AREN'T THE ONLY ONES WHO KNOW HOW TO DUCK AND ROLL!
HEY! ISN'T ANYONE GOING TO COMMENT ON MY BIG SAVE?

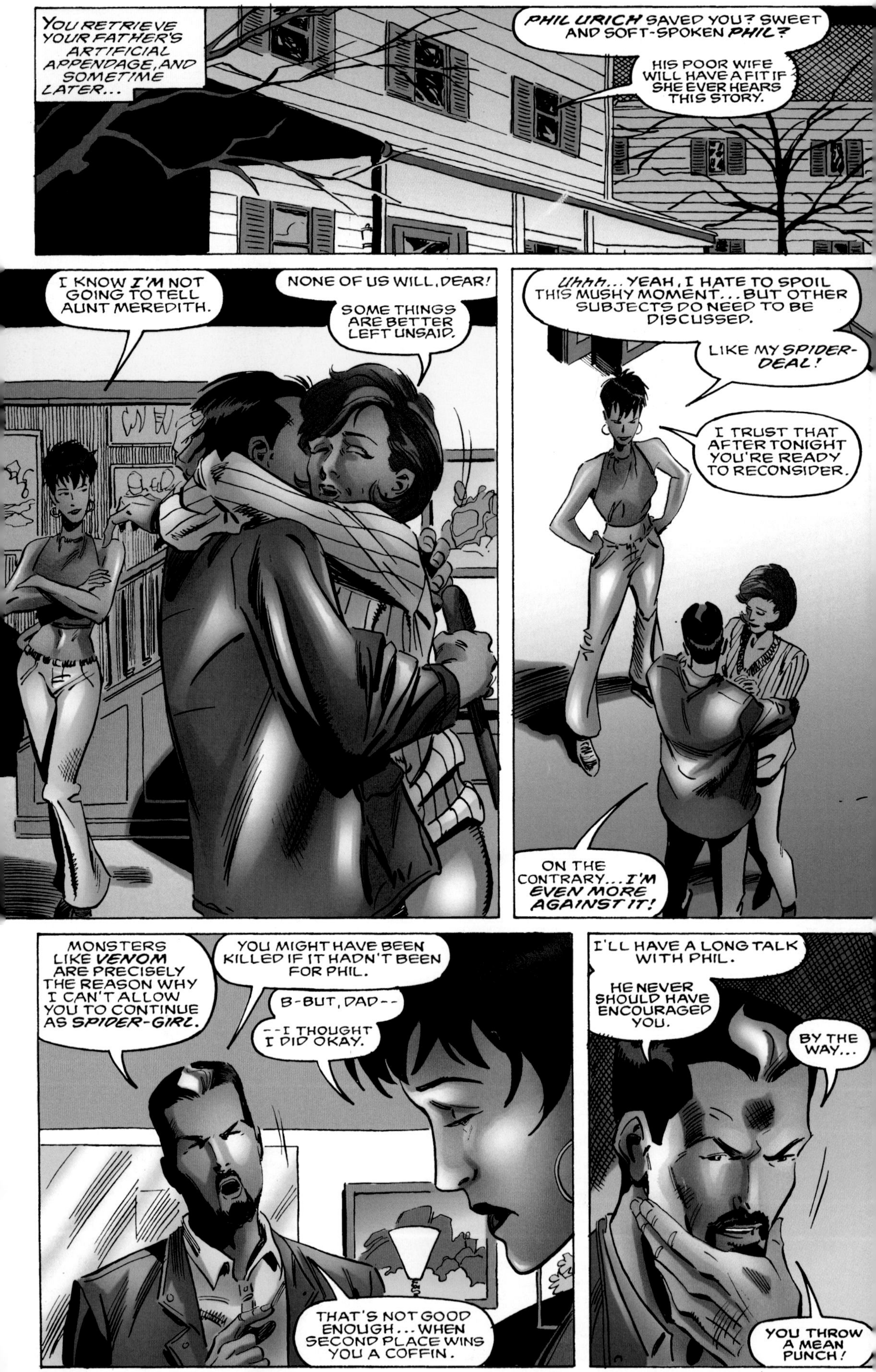

YOU RETRIEVE YOUR FATHER'S ARTIFICIAL APPENDAGE, AND SOMETIME LATER...
PHIL URICH SAVED YOU? SWEET AND SOFT-SPOKEN *PHIL*?
HIS POOR WIFE WILL HAVE A FIT IF SHE EVER HEARS THIS STORY.
I KNOW *I'M* NOT GOING TO TELL AUNT MEREDITH.
NONE OF US WILL, DEAR!
SOME THINGS ARE BETTER LEFT UNSAID.
Uhhh... YEAH, I HATE TO SPOIL THIS MUSHY MOMENT... BUT OTHER SUBJECTS DO NEED TO BE DISCUSSED.
LIKE MY *SPIDER-DEAL*!
I TRUST THAT AFTER TONIGHT YOU'RE READY TO RECONSIDER.
ON THE CONTRARY... *I'M EVEN MORE AGAINST IT!*
MONSTERS LIKE *VENOM* ARE PRECISELY THE REASON WHY I CAN'T ALLOW YOU TO CONTINUE AS *SPIDER-GIRL*.
YOU MIGHT HAVE BEEN KILLED IF IT HADN'T BEEN FOR PHIL.
B-BUT, DAD--
--I THOUGHT I DID OKAY.
THAT'S NOT GOOD ENOUGH... WHEN SECOND PLACE WINS YOU A COFFIN.
I'LL HAVE A LONG TALK WITH PHIL.
HE NEVER SHOULD HAVE ENCOURAGED YOU.
BY THE WAY...
YOU THROW A MEAN PUNCH!

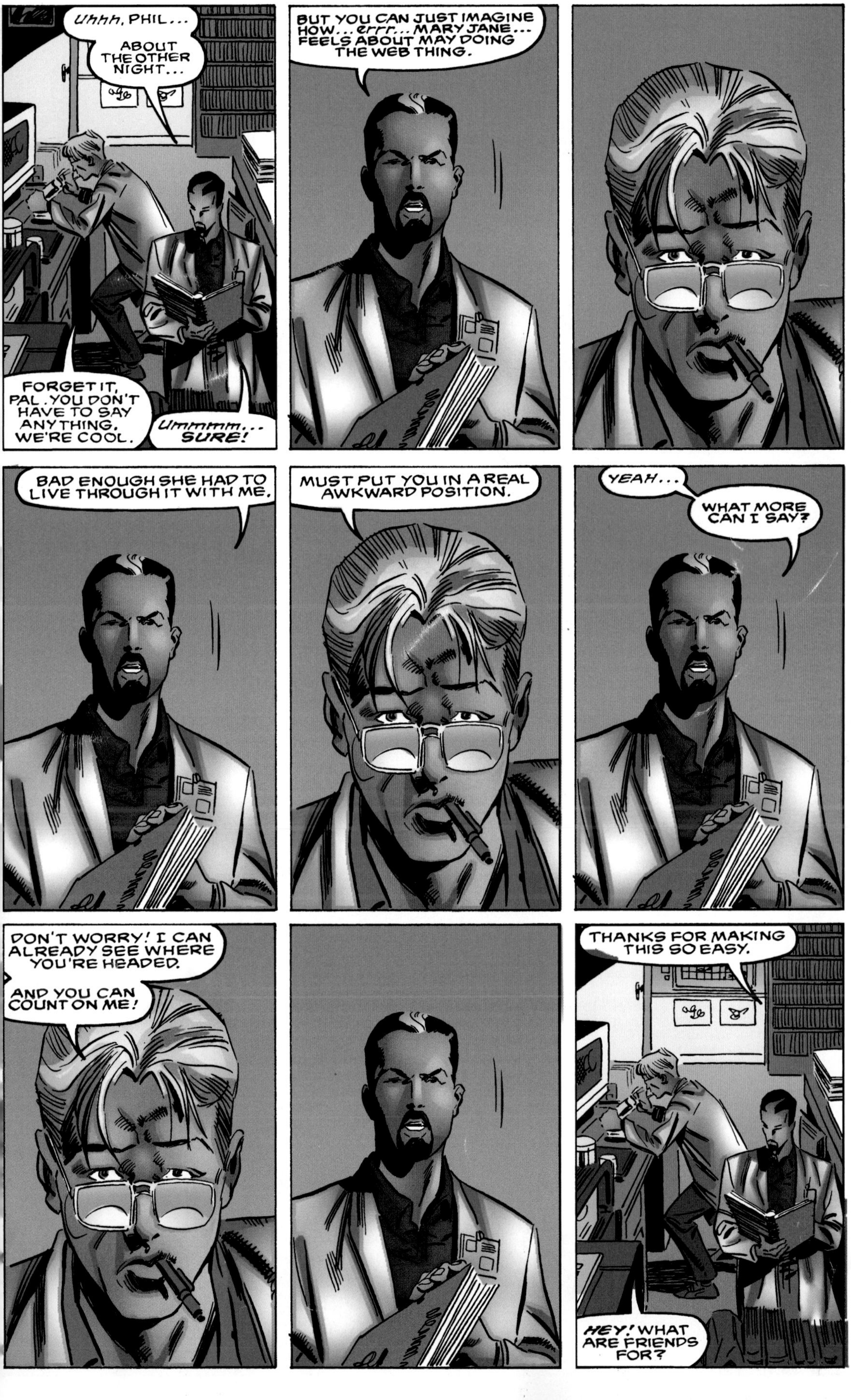

UHHH, PHIL...
ABOUT THE OTHER NIGHT...
FORGET IT, PAL. YOU DON'T HAVE TO SAY ANYTHING. WE'RE COOL.
UMMMMM... SURE!
BUT YOU CAN JUST IMAGINE HOW... ERRR... MARY JANE... FEELS ABOUT MAY DOING THE WEB THING.
BAD ENOUGH SHE HAD TO LIVE THROUGH IT WITH ME.
MUST PUT YOU IN A REAL AWKWARD POSITION.
YEAH...
WHAT MORE CAN I SAY?
DON'T WORRY! I CAN ALREADY SEE WHERE YOU'RE HEADED.
AND YOU CAN COUNT ON ME!
THANKS FOR MAKING THIS SO EASY.
HEY! WHAT ARE FRIENDS FOR?

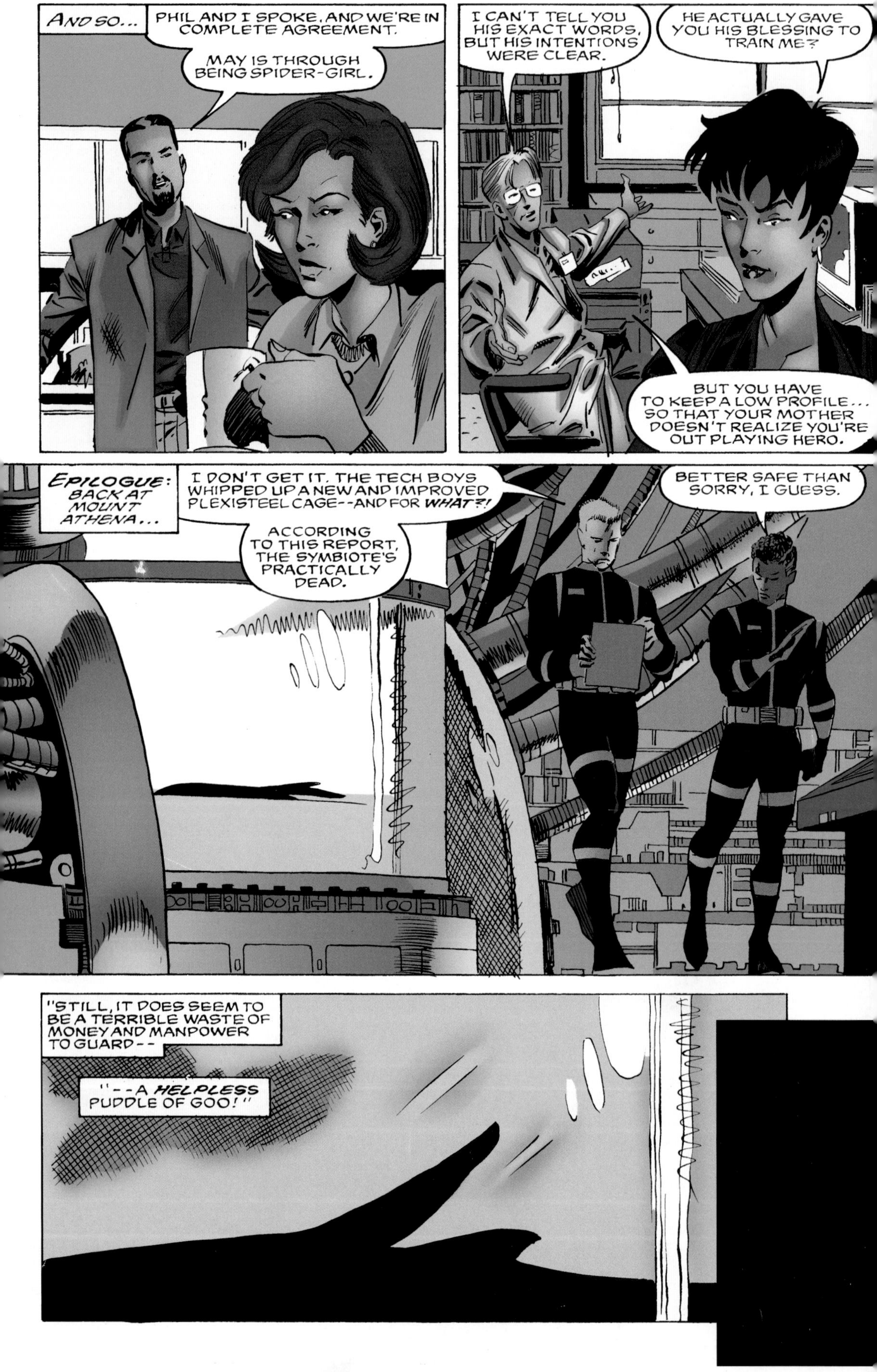
AND SO...
PHIL AND I SPOKE, AND WE'RE IN COMPLETE AGREEMENT.
MAY IS THROUGH BEING SPIDER-GIRL.
I CAN'T TELL YOU HIS EXACT WORDS, BUT HIS INTENTIONS WERE CLEAR.
HE ACTUALLY GAVE YOU HIS BLESSING TO TRAIN ME?
BUT YOU HAVE TO KEEP A LOW PROFILE... SO THAT YOUR MOTHER DOESN'T REALIZE YOU'RE OUT PLAYING HERO.
EPILOGUE: BACK AT MOUNT ATHENA...
I DON'T GET IT. THE TECH BOYS WHIPPED UP A NEW AND IMPROVED PLEXISTEEL CAGE--AND FOR WHAT?!
ACCORDING TO THIS REPORT, THE SYMBIOTE'S PRACTICALLY DEAD.
BETTER SAFE THAN SORRY, I GUESS.
"STILL, IT DOES SEEM TO BE A TERRIBLE WASTE OF MONEY AND MANPOWER TO GUARD--
"--A HELPLESS PUDDLE OF GOO!"